OP 10/07

D1505677

WORD BIRD
MAKES WORDS WITH DUCK

by Jane Belk Moncure
illustrated by Linda Hohag

THE
CHILD'S
WORLD

MANKATO, MN 56001

We acknowledge with gratitude the review of the Word Bird Short Vowel Adventure *books by Dr. John Mize, Director of Reading, Alamance County Schools, Graham, North Carolina.*

—The Child's World

Library of Congress Cataloging in Publication Data

Moncure, Jane Belk.
  Word Bird makes words with Duck.
  — A short "u" adventure.

  (Word Bird's short vowel adventures)
  Summary: On a rainy day Word Bird makes up words with his friend Duck. Each word that they make up leads them into a new activity.
  [1. Vocabulary. 2. Birds—Fiction. 3. Ducks—Fiction] I. Hohag, Linda, ill. II. Title.
  III. Series: Moncure, Jane Belk. Word Bird's short vowel adventures.
  PZ7.M739Wne 1984   [E]   83-23943
  ISBN 0-89565-261-7 -1991 Edition

WORD BIRD
MAKES WORDS WITH DUCK

One rainy day Word
Bird made word
puzzles

under an
umbrella.

WORD
PUZZLES

He put

d with uck

What word did Word Bird make?

d uck

5

Just then his friend
Duck came to play.

"I can make word puzzles too," said Duck.

She put

s with un

What word did Duck make?

s un

Just then the sun
came out.

Word Bird put down
the umbrella.

But then the thunder rumbled.

So Word Bird put up the umbrella again.

"What can we do?"
asked Duck.

Word Bird made another
word. He put

dr with um

What word did he make?

dr um

10

"I have a drum," said Word Bird.

"Let's play your drum," said Duck. They played. Tum-tum-tum. Tum-tum-tum.

The thunder rumbled.
Bum-bum.

And tum-tum went
the drum.

Then the sun came out.

Word Bird put down the umbrella again.

"What can we do now?"
asked Duck.

Word Bird made another
word.

He put

tr with uck

What word did he
make?

tr uck

"Let's play with my truck," said Word Bird. "I have a dump truck."

Duck found a mud puddle.

"Let's put mud in the dump truck," she said.

They filled the dump truck with mud. Then they dumped the mud.

"Let's make mud pies,"
said Duck.

They made lots of mud pies. "The sun will dry the mud pies," said Duck.

"Let's jump over the mud puddle," said Word Bird. But...

...he jumped into the mud!

Word Bird was stuck
in the mud.

Duck pulled him out.

"You must jump very high so you will not get stuck in the mud," said Duck.

Suddenly it began to thunder again. So Word Bird put up the umbrella.

"What can we do now?" asked Duck.

Word Bird put...

What word did he make?

"I have a little bus,"
said Word Bird.

"I will be the bus
driver," he said.

"No, no!" said Duck. "I will be the bus driver."

Then they had a fuss.

"Let's take turns," said
Word Bird. "You drive
the bus. Then I will drive
the bus."

The bus went bump
bump.

Duck stopped the bus.
Word Bird jumped out.
He picked a bunch of
buttercups for Duck.

And Duck gave Word
Bird a hug.

You can read these  puzzles.

b ug

c up

r ug

f un

g un

t ug

l umpy

gr umpy

t ub

d umpy

b umpy

j umpy

Now you make some word puzzles.